# Sammy's Hamburger Caper

KAEDEN BOOKS

D1403534

written by:  Kathleen Urmston
Craig Urmston
illustrated by:  Gloria Gedeon

Sammy was next to Dad's chair
trying to sleep.

Sarah and Will were tickling Sammy's paws and blowing in his ears.

They wouldn't leave him alone.

Suddenly Sammy jumped up,
ran to the kitchen and crawled
under the table.

"Sammy! Here Sammy!" the
children called.

"Hey Mom,
have you seen
Sammy?"

5

"No," said Mom as she put the hamburgers on the table for lunch.

"Please go wash your hands. We are ready for lunch."

Sammy smelled the hamburgers.

He crawled out from under the table.

He sniffed around and around the table.

"No! No!" said Mom to Sammy.

Mom called to Dad,
"Time for lunch."

"I will be right there," said Dad.

Mom waited.  No one came.

Mom went to the living room.

Everyone was playing a video game.

"Oh no! The hamburgers!" shouted
Mom as she ran to the kitchen.

Dad ran to the kitchen.

Sarah and Will ran to the
kitchen too.

Sammy was under the table. The tablecloth was on the floor. The broken dishes were on the floor. The hamburger buns were on the floor too. All of the hamburgers were gone. Sammy was licking the floor.

Sammy let out a loud

"Burp!"

Sammy knew he was in big trouble. He jumped up to run.

Dad grabbed for his tail. Sarah and Will grabbed for his feet. Mom grabbed for his collar. Mom picked up Sammy and put him outside.

Everyone cleaned up the mess.
"Pizza anyone?" said Dad.